THE RAVEN'S DAUGHTER

Tales of the Ravensdaughter
- Adventure Six

Erin Hunt Rado

D1736077

For my beloved Paul
And thank you Caitlyn Johnston for some cool ideas!

The children who knew shadows
Have risen now to fame.
They know their place and power.
They know their true acclaim.

Regard them now, these Walkers,
Gods above and gods below.
The Realme has kissed Mortalia
Forever now, and long ago.

- from the Scrolls of Imari

The dawn's wind blew briskly across Alerice's cheek and tossed her blonde hair about her eyes. She shivered and drew her feathered cloak closer, for the chill chasing down her back was not borne of the wind.

The sights and sounds of two armies filled her senses. She could feel their wild energy, like two great beasts about to tear into one another. She could smell the dirt churned up by men's boots, horses' hooves, and wagon wheels. She could hear voices, some shouting, some an underlying drone.

Alerice had thought the task assigned by the Raven Queen would be simpler. She had commanded that Alerice retrieve as many souls as she could, and deliver them to the Hall of Eternity so they might be processed without guiding them in from the Convergence.

The queen had gifted her the feathered cloak for this purpose. Just as with the cloak belonging to one of the Raven Knights that Alerice had worn in the town of Uffton, she would be able to fly about the battlefield and tuck souls into the winged fabric. She would be able to dart and flit so quickly that she doubted any of the fighting men would be able to see her, let alone land a blow against her.

All the same, in addition to her black scale mail tunic, she now wore black metal leg plates along with the black gorget and pauldrons that Oddwyn had offered her when he, and she, had first outfitted her.

Alerice also bore a helm, which she tucked into

the crook of her arm. Similar to a Raven Knight's, hers was fashioned in the shape of a bird's skull with a spray of metal feathers rising from the top-back of the crestline.

However, unlike a knight's helm, her visor was open. Alerice was grateful for this because she had never worn a helm before. She had never worn full armor before, and for that matter, she had never seen the dreadful sight of two massive groups of men about to destroy one another.

"Pretty sight," Kreston said from behind.

Alerice turned about to find him standing at her flank, the vanishing traces of a Realme portal dissolving in the tri-colors of black, midnight blue, and deep teal.

Kreston was dressed in gray scales, and Alerice paused, for this was the first time she had seen him in armor. His tunic looked as though it had been crafted by the King of Shadows, for it was not a solid color. Depending on how Kreston moved, the metal shifted from light to dark gray, save for one red patch on his upper left chest.

Alerice did not know the reason for this mark, and she did not wish to inquire. She surmised that, in the heat of battle, it could draw an opponent's focus to Kreston's left side, allowing him to strike from the right.

However, it could also be a reminder of his lost Crimson Brigade, and this was not a subject Alerice was about to broach.

The remainder of Kreston's body was protected by plate. As with the king's Shadow Warriors, his leg and arm plates were etched with wispy curls. So too were his pauldrons, which bore metal spikes resembling the crystals protruding from the shoulders of the King of Shadows' own long robe.

Kreston's helm, which he too held in the crook of his arm, was a single piece with angled, open eye slits and an angled nose guard. The front slit was long and pointed. Upon the brow rested an off-set square that bore two crossed red broadswords. Alerice somehow knew that this must be the badge of Kreston's lost Crimsons. Indeed, any fighting man seeing him so adorned would instantly recognize him as the ghost of that tragic regiment.

Alerice watched as Kreston looked past her to survey the battlefield. They both stood some distance away on a small rise topped by a little shade tree. His expression belied the ice that she had seen him summon into his veins. His hazel eyes were hard. His demeanor reminded her of when they had fought creatures in the Evherealme, that of a man capable of wholesale slaughter. With what Oddwyn had told her of Kreston's history – and especially now that the Raven Queen had unlocked his mind – Alerice sensed that the King of Shadows had assigned Kreston the task of killing as many men as he could.

Kreston's eyes shifted to her, and she lifted her chin a bit. She held his gaze for a moment, but then saw him draw a thin breath before his shoulders lowered.

He tossed his helm so that it turned upside down, and caught its crown in his gray-gloved palm. He placed it on his head with practiced ease, and looked again at the field.

"Stay clear of me," he warned.

"Because the king has sent you to claim souls, just as the queen has sent me?"

"Because the king has sent me to do what I do best, and I don't want you getting in the way."

Alerice looked over her shoulder at the armies. "I take it that the king enjoys this type of entertainment."

Kreston humphed. "Are you joking? This is what he *lives* for."

Alerice turned to the field as Kreston stepped up to her side.

"I'm not going to let you ruin yourself," she said.

"Too late."

"I'm serious, Kreston," she said, turning her head to him. "I meant what I told the King of Shadows. I am going to be your advocate."

"Huzzah to that."

Alerice did not wish to suffer sarcasm at a time like this, and so she tucked her intentions to the back of her mind and looked at the forming lines. Then, she focused on the standards of both armies, and concern crept into her thoughts.

One army bore the standard of her home city of Navre: four golden circles on a blue field. The other bore the standard of Navre's sister city, A'Leon: a white lion on a blue field.

"This isn't right," she said.

"If only I had a gold coin for every time I've heard you say that."

Alerice shot Kreston a scorned look, but he simply stared ahead. Seeing that he was not about to engage, she continued.

"Why would Navre and A'Leon fight one another? Their Prime Chevals are brothers, Lord Andoni and Lord Bolivar."

"Sibling rivalry?" Kreston suggested.

"Stop it, Kreston. I've lived in Navre since I was five. There is simply no way that those two would fight one another."

Horns blew and the roar of men rose up. Alerice shivered once more, but Kreston's gloved hand caught hold of her upper arm to steady her.

"Just fly fast," he said. "The way you did in Uffton."

Alerice's brow wrinkled. "How did you know I did that? You weren't with me then. You had already left Uffton."

Kreston did not reply, except to repeat, "Fly fast."

With that, Kreston charged so quickly that Alerice had difficulty tracking him. He bolted straight for the armies, drawing the King of Shadows' broadsword as he hurried toward the thick of the fight.

Then, as the first blows landed and the first men cried out in agony, Alerice felt her spine straighten of its own accord. She felt her feathered cloak spread out, and felt it bear her down into a waiting crouch.

Alerice hastily donned her helmet, for in the next moment her body sprang forward from the little rise and its lone shade tree, her cloak spreading into wings as she, too, shot for the thick of the fray.

There was no time to think, no time to reason or analyze. There were only lightning-fast flits from body to body and soul to soul.

Somehow, Alerice recalled what Oddwyn had ordered in Uffton when the faun souls were facing the dangers of the morning sunlight.

"'Gods above, Alerice. You're a Realme Walker,'" he had said. "'One of your tasks will always be shepherding souls into the Realme. Now hurry before you lose them.'"

Alerice had spread her wings back then, and darted with surprising deftness. She did so now, reaching out to catch hold of any nearby soul that rose away from its corpse, and tucking it safely within the metaphysical folds of her black feathers.

She felt as small as a sparrow, nimbly shifting course from wingbeat to wingbeat. She moved by will, her consciousness guiding her cloak to propel her forward.

She saw a Navre foot soldier gasp and collapse. His soul shot from his body as surely as if it had been cast from a sling. She caught hold of its shoulder and tucked it to her side as she might catch a coin from one of her old tavern customers and tuck it in her purse.

The wind rushed past her face, venting into her helm, and though her eyes narrowed, she retained full sight of the work at hand.

Swordsmen, axemen, and pikemen, Alerice flew above and about them as a black angel, securing souls by any means, whether they required tugging up from their mortal remains as she might tug up roots from a garden, or capturing them in erratic flight, as she might take hold of a moth desperate to escape a window pane.

Alerice did not know how many souls her cloak could bear. The Raven Queen had told her that when the cloak had reached a full tally, it would feel heavier and slow her flight.

Indeed, this did happen after what seemed a good amount of time, but from what Alerice could see of the battle below, it had not been much time at all. The men below were still hotly engaged with no signs of slowing.

"My Queen!" she called as she banked to double-back upon her last direction.

As Alerice looked ahead, she could see a Realme portal opening midair. She flew straight toward it, but as she glanced down she saw Kreston cutting, thrusting, and slicing through any nearby body, and she felt a pang of heartache for him.

Alerice flew into the Hall of Eternity. She had no idea how to land, and she crashed and tumbled forward, her plated knees striking the floor's great mosaic glyphs. Some of the amorphous spirit guides, who guided souls from the Convergence, rushed to her side. They removed her cloak and shook it out as servants might shake out the dust from a long journey.

Alerice looked up to find the Raven Queen floating toward her, and she rose to all fours and shook her head to regain her senses. She saw the Raven Queen gesture 'up' with her willow-white hand, and Alerice felt an unseen force gently help her to her feet. There, she readied her stance, for the queen was opening another portal to the battlefield.

As the spirit guides replaced the cloak about her shoulders, Alerice felt it prepare her to spring back into action, but she quickly looked about.

"Where's Oddwyn?"

"In the Convergence," the queen replied.

Alerice looked into her matron's pale face, drawing strength from her deep amethyst gaze. She nodded, ready to continue, but paused as the Raven Queen advised, "Approach with your feet before you, Alerice. Just as a bird might do."

Alerice nodded and launched herself through the waiting portal.

Alerice's second flight mirrored her first, but with many more souls to collect now that the battle was fully joined. She concentrated on those that appeared to be the most confounded, unaccepting of what had just happened to them.

Some reached out to her willingly. Some resisted her, and she had to fight to catch hold of them and tuck them into her cloak. She felt the latter kick within her feathers like a prisoner when the door slams shut, but the commotion died down quickly enough for Alerice to lift more men away from the sad world that had seen their lives' end.

Then, as she circled the heart of the conflict, she saw Kreston raise his broadsword and heard him shout, "My King!" His broadsword glowed brightly, causing men to shrink from him. She saw a Realme portal open for him, and he jumped through.

Wanting to fully understand his task, Alerice collected as many souls as were handy, and then flew back toward the short rise and its lone, little shade tree.

"My Queen!" she shouted.

As she hoped, a portal opened for her and she flew through.

This time, Alerice imagined the wild bird she used to feed when she managed the Cup and Quill. It was a pretty boy with a red breast and tan wings tipped in black. She used to place crumbs on her window sill and watch it alight to peck. She now employed that seemingly mundane observation to her advantage as she expended her legs before her so that her boot soles struck the Hall of Eternity's glyph-encrusted floor.

She landed on balance, and stood as the spirit guides came to collect her cloak. They shook it out as before, and while they shooed the exiting souls toward a waiting area near the side of the dais below the queen's throne, Alerice looked over her shoulder to find Kreston kneeling before the King of Shadows.

He extended his broadsword, which the king grasped in both hands. Then, as though drawing from a long pipe, the king inhaled the souls trapped in the steel.

His dark gray eyes widened, and his face flashed with exhilarated ferocity. He hooted and slapped his chest, and for a moment, Alerice thought he might expel a burst of power that would demolish his side of the hall.

"More!" the king shouted.

Kreston nodded and stood, taking back the broadsword and holding it ready.

Alerice saw him look at her, his hazel eyes meeting hers for the briefest moment. Then he turned and stepped through the portal that the King of Shadows had opened for him.

"Alerice," the Raven Queen said.

Alerice's face snapped to her matron's. The queen regarded the king, and Alerice saw in her expression the same suppressed anger that she had seen in many a disappointed wife come to collect their drunken husbands from the Cup and Quill.

"You may stop Kreston, if you can," the queen said softly. "But do not allow your concern for him to hinder your task. The more souls you deliver to me, the fewer for Oddwyn to sort in the Convergence... and the fewer for my husband to devour."

Alerice nodded as she prepared to take flight a third time.

Alerice again circled the center of the battlefield, for the fighting along the sidelines had become sporadic skirmishes in which few men perished. Again, she saw Kreston in the heart of the conflict, but despite possessing a Realme Walker's enhanced stamina, he was beginning to show signs of fatigue. Even so, men dared not approach him, and the only combatants he could slay were the unfortunate ones who ventured too close.

Alerice could see that a great deal of momentum had dissipated in both armies, and though she could see that more men wore white lions than gold circles, it seemed to her that the two armies had fought themselves into a stalemate.

Then a shout of "For Andoni!" rang out from a mounted A'Leon captain, which Alerice found strange. Andoni was the Prime Cheval of Navre. It made no sense that anyone from A'Leon would use his name as a battle cry.

A small cavalry unit repeated the call before they followed the captain into the final pit of activity.

They were heading directly toward Kreston.

Alerice rolled off to her left and dove down to intercept them as Kreston prepared to fend them off.

As she soared low, the A'Leon foot soldiers closed in, some even drawing up the courage to approach Kreston from behind.

Alerice swooped in as a blackened *whoosh*, and the foot soldiers leaped back, even as Kreston half-turned in their direction. He held his broadsword aloft and yelled at the top of his lungs. The soldiers scurried away as Kreston quickly turned back to the incoming cavalry. However, with a reverse swoop, Alerice brushed past the lead horse. It reared and whinnied, throwing the captain to the mud.

Kreston stalked toward the downed officer, and Alerice had only an instant to stop him. She reversed direction once again to fly in low, and pushed Kreston backward before he could strike.

The remaining horses either reared or sidled into one another, fouling the charge and frustrating the cavalry. A hush fell over the field, and Alerice *whooshed* past Kreston once more, making certain that her cloak brushed the faces of as many men as possible.

"Damn it, Alerice!" she heard Kreston shout. However, his consternation made her smirk, for by denying him combat she was doing what she had promised the King of Shadows she would do: become Kreston's advocate. He would slaughter no more men this day.

Though her cloak required unburdening, Alerice banked about, extended her legs, and set her boots down into the mud. She steadied herself, and employing the old trick of bending her knees to maintain balance, she straightened her back and struck a stance, shoulders squared and head high.

"Stand down, Crimson Ghost!" she ordered.

Through his helm's angled eye slits, Alerice saw Kreston blink in astonishment. "What?" he exclaimed.

"Can you not hear me? I said stand down!" she demanded.

Alerice held her ground, but then Kreston snarled and raised his broadsword. She leaped aside, her cloak carrying her well out of his range, and drew the pixie pole cylinders from her belt. She caused the bladed poles to appear, and noted that the men about her murmured in astonishment and gave her room.

She faced Kreston, whose fatigue was becoming more apparent, and knowing that she needed to extract them both to the safety of the Realme, she *clanged* her poles together. The clear tone rang out, and several men recoiled.

Kreston cried out and turned his body away while raising a hand in surrender.

"Mercy, Ravensdaughter," he panted, his voice loud enough for all to hear. "The Ghost of the Crimson Brigade yields to you."

Alerice did not know how to respond, and so she *clanged* her poles again. She caused the mark of the Raven Queen to glow upon her brow, emitting an odd purplish light within her helm. She watched more men back away, which afforded her a few precious moments.

"My Queen!" she called mentally. She looked about for a portal, but did not see one forming. Hoping no one would try to claim an advantage while she closed her eyes, Alerice gave her entire being over to her mark. She felt her way through time and space as she visualized the Realme's mossy rise surrounded by columns where Oddwyn had once taken her to be healed.

"My Queen!" she called again, praying that her matron would deliver her and Kreston to safety without delay.

Distant thunder rolled across the sky. Alerice sensed it more than she heard it, but then she heard something that she did not expect – a man's deep, far-off laughter.

"L'Orku," men muttered, ruining her concentration. Alerice opened her eyes and looked about. Kreston recovered and moved close to her side as more men looked skyward and murmured, "L'Orku."

Kreston took hold of her arm and leaned in close to whisper, "They're hoping the thunder god joins them tonight."

Alerice glanced at Kreston and then regarded the men, for she recalled the army lore her father had once imparted, that if L'Orku and his brother Gäete, God of Storms, assumed human disguises and sat at a regiment's campfire, no harm would befall the men that night and no rain would fall upon the battlefield.

The laughter faded, but then lightning tore across the sky. Thunder *boomed*, startling some, and as the din rolled away, a man's voice proclaimed, "Hail to the Ravensdaughter!"

Alerice watched at least a hundred men turn to her, sending a shiver up her spine. She had never felt more exposed in her life.

"Hail to the Ravensdaughter," a few men echoed, somewhat stupefied. "Hail," more said with mounting confidence. "Hail," even more joined in until all nearby began to raise their weapons and call, "Hail to the Ravensdaughter."

The cavalry captain, half-covered in mud, came forward. He stopped before Alerice and saluted, then turned to his men and shouted, "Hail to the Ravensdaughter! She has vanquished the Ghost of the Crimson Brigade!"

Alerice cringed internally, and pressed a bit closer to Kreston. He shoved her forward and took a knee at her side, burying the point of his broadsword into the soil and gripping its handle with both hands. Then he bowed the crown of his helm onto the pommel.

Alerice wanted to kick him to make him stand up, but just then she saw something that she truly could not believe. A rider drew near, bearing the Navre standard. Next two men rode forth.

One was the Reef of Navre, the same villain who had stabbed her on the open road and sent her body to the Realme. The second was none other than her rapist, Mayor Gotthard, who now wore the trappings of Navre's Prime Cheval.

The poisoned cup she had given Gotthard had apparently not killed him, and since Lord Andoni was nowhere to be found, it suddenly struck Alerice why men of A'Leon were calling Andoni's name. If Gotthard had assumed Andoni's place, it was a simple matter for Alerice to conclude that Gotthard had murdered Andoni in a rise to power.

"My Queen!" Alerice shouted aloud. "Great Lady Raven! I claim my prize for the Evherealme!" she said, grabbing hold of Kreston's vambrace and tugging for him to rise.

He did, and to Alerice's great relief she saw a portal open before her. Men gasped as it swirled in black, midnight blue, and deep teal, and she caught one final glimpse of the Reef's and Gotthard's astonished looks as she guided Kreston into the safety of the world below.

***

"Kreston, will you just support yourself against the column?" Alerice asked. She lifted Kreston's arm and guided his hand to the column's surface, exposing the side of his body so that she could begin unbuckling the leather straps of his scale mail tunic.

"I can get out of my own gear."

She paused and straightened to look at him. "I know you can, but you're tired, and you can't honestly look me in the eye and tell me that you don't appreciate my help."

She watched him try, but in the end he smiled and humphed a little laugh. She smiled back, and returned to her task.

They stood on the mossy rise where the 'sky' above swirled in tones of deep teal with light blue currents creating a daylight hue.

They had already been to the Hall of Eternity where the spirit guides had taken her cloak to shake the souls free. The Raven Queen had recalled Oddwyn from the Convergence, where Alerice learned that he had been more than occupied sorting the souls that Alerice had not been able to gather. There was also the natural influx of souls from other Mortalia deaths, so battles were indeed intense times for the Realme.

The queen had instructed Oddwyn to help Alerice out of her helm and plate, but given that the King of Shadows had engorged himself on the final souls Kreston had taken, there was no one to tend to his needs, and so Alerice had asked that the Raven Queen send them both to this place where she might see to Kreston herself.

The column was composed of the same silver-veined stone that formed the Convergence's arches, and Kreston had placed his hand over one of the black glyphs. A cascade of silvery glimmers flowed down about his fingertips from the column's crown, and Alerice could sense that he was already beginning to relax from his exertion. She gave thanks to any gods that might be listening that he had not suffered serious injury.

She moved to Kreston's other side and finished unbuckling his scales. Then she helped lift the tunic over his head and set it down. She noted that he watched with pleasant satisfaction as she began to unbuckle his arm plates. Then she tended to his leg plates, unbuckling them and untying them from his gambeson so she could also set them atop his scales.

She guided Kreston to recline on the moss, and then sat down next to him.

"Keeping your scales on?" he asked.

"For now," she said.

"Mmmm," he muttered, his hazel eyes fluttering even though he tried to keep them open.

"I wish I could put you to sleep," she said, stroking his salt-and-pepper hair. "If I had a potion to give you, I would. I'm just glad that those horses didn't ride over you. They, and the men coming up on your back, could have killed you."

"You should have let them."

"Don't say that, Kreston."

"Why not? It wouldn't have been the first time I died in *his* service."

Alerice noted the derisive manner in which Kreston referred to the King of Shadows. He used to use that tone when referring to the Raven Queen, but now that his mind was free, he knew where to focus his resentment.

"I don't want you to die," she said.

"It would have gotten me out of there."

"I got you out of there. And I'll keep doing so as long as the king sends you to slaughter people."

"Which," he said sleepily, "makes you dangerous."

"How so?" she asked.

He smiled as he gazed up at her. He stroked a lock of her blonde hair, and ran his fingertips along the burn scar that Sukaar, Father God of Fire, had left upon her jaw. Then he sighed and flopped his arm onto his chest.

"Later," he exhaled.

His eyes closed and he began to drift off. Alerice wanted to kiss him, but she was afraid that would imply a promise she did not wish to keep. She thought about kissing his brow where the King of Shadows had scratched his mark into Kreston's skin, but that would be making the same promise.

She decided to pet his head. Then she looked about at the mossy rise, and the columns, and their sparkles cascading down from their tops like glistening little waterfalls.

Alerice saw the maiden Oddwyn standing a small ways off. She brightened at the sight of her Realme sister and waved, taking care not to disturb Kreston. Oddwyn waved back, and beckoned for her to come over. Alerice slowly slid away from Kreston's side to join her.

Alerice and Oddwyn walked for a short while, saying nothing. As she kept her eyes down, Alerice occasionally caught sight of the hem of Oddwyn's iridescent belted demi-gown that showed off her light-blue leggings and white boots.

The path they treaded was made of midnight blue paving stones, and currents of pewter-gray ether undulated on both sides. The path seemed to go on forever while leading nowhere. It was yet another mystery of the Evherealme that Alerice was pleased to discover.

"The king is going to be furious at Kreston when I tell him that he yielded to you," Oddwyn said.

"He doesn't already know?" Alerice asked.

"I think he's had too many souls," Oddwyn said.

Alerice nodded, but then asked, "Can't you tell him that Kreston simply withdrew from the field?"

Oddwyn smiled knowingly. "The Ghost of the Crimson Brigade does not 'withdraw from the field'. He either clears the field or dies on it. If he dies, the king doesn't get his fill. Kreston's soul comes into the Convergence, and the king takes hold of it. I fetch Kreston's body, and the king melds the two together. Either way, the king always asks me how the battle went, and I always have to tell him."

Alerice patted her hand on her thigh. "I'm not certain why Kreston did yield. He could have defeated me if he had attacked me. He knows that."

Oddwyn stopped and turned to Alerice. "You're not serious. Why did he yield? Because he loves you, Alerice, and he had to find a way to avoid fighting you without losing face. Luckily, you've learned to use your cloak, and you put on quite a show, calling him the Crimson Ghost. It's natural that things of the Realme should come quickly to you now. Your soul is nearly tethered here."

"Tethered," Alerice pondered.

"Does that worry you?"

"I don't know. It doesn't feel bad, but I'm not certain if it feels right. I'm still mortal. How will I manage myself?"

"Oh, you'll manage yourself. You can manage anything. I see that now. And so does the queen."

"And the king?" Alerice asked.

After a pause, Oddwyn answered, "Yep. Kreston is right. You're dangerous."

"But I don't wish to be."

"But what choice will you have, Alerice? When things are dire and you wish to follow your own mind, especially when it comes to Kreston? Do you think the King of Shadows is going to stand by and let you rob him of his prized Realme Walker? He keeps Kreston as a gem, just as the queen kept her Eye."

Oddwyn turned and began walking along their path again. "But that's not why I wanted to speak to you. Over the ages, I have known several Realme Walkers. Not many, because you people aren't born that often, but a few. However, I've never met a Walker like you. Perhaps it was the way you were born, or the gods who might have been involved, who knows? But you are almost able to open your own portal, and Walkers can't do that. I said you were becoming tethered. There's a way you can control how it happens. You've been kissed by the Raven Queen, but there's another kiss that will bind you to us forever."

"The king's," Alerice said, knowing this as surely as she knew herself.

"Mm hmm," Oddwyn said. "If he kisses you, the duality is complete."

"What about if you kissed me?" Alerice teased.

Oddwyn presented himself as a youth, and placed a hand on Alerice's arm. She stopped and turned to him – but then he stepped in and kissed her. He wrapped his arms about her black scales and she found herself wrapping her arms around his iridescent tunic. Their kiss was deep and lasting, and they felt their spirits mingle.

When it ended, their lips parted and they both found themselves out of breath. They swooned, and soon began to steady one another.

"That was good!" he exclaimed.

"Yes, it was," Alerice commented.

"Whoof," Oddwyn said, his head lolling as the little bursts of color in his white hair gleamed. Eventually, he recovered and looked into her eyes. "Feel like a demi-goddess?"

"Mmmm, not particularly."

"Well, it's obviously not my kiss that you require. It's the king's, and the thing is, he knows what his kiss will do to you, so you should be prepared that he might see it as his only means to control you, if he doesn't lash out at you first."

"But he doesn't need to lash out or control me, Oddwyn. Neither of them do."

Oddwyn presented herself as a maiden once again, and continued in her soft voice, "Alerice, I'm going to let you in on a truth. The only thing that the king and queen have to call their own is control. Look about you. This is the Evherealme. It's not a land of hope. It's a land of memory. All the souls here had their chance to live. Some did well. Some did horribly. But that time is past.

"Mortalia is the world of hope, and dreams, and all the happy things people conjure up. Mortals are alive to live out those things, for good or ill, and it is life's unpredictability that proffers multiple outcomes.

"Here, things are fixed. Here things are shadows of what they once were. Here, the King of Shadows and the Raven Queen have one thing: control over who gets which souls, how they dispose of those souls, and how they maintain this world of souls.

"And now the queen has an advantage," Oddwyn added. "You. Kreston is spent. There's no hiding it. He has a few years left, but he's ebbing. You, on the other hand, are ascending. You are a wonder to behold, a strange dichotomy of modesty and pride.

"But there's one more thing that makes all this truly interesting," Oddwyn said. "You have also been kissed by two gods above, Sukaar, Father Fire, and Imari, Mother Water Wind, and if the king kisses you to complete our duality, their duality might allow you to transcend what either the Raven Queen or the

King of Shadows thinks you're capable of."

"That is interesting," Alerice commented. "Do you think the king or queen have considered this?"

"I have no idea what they consider. It's not my place to know their minds."

Alerice was tempted to challenge this point, given Oddwyn's constant attendance upon the Realme's mistress, but her matter-of-fact response made Alerice think twice.

"Oddwyn," she said. "If I chose to solicit the king's kiss, do you think he would grant it?"

"I don't know. As I said, he's going to be furious when he learns what Kreston did." Oddwyn presented himself once more as a youth and asked, "Does this mean you are thinking of binding yourself here?"

"I am, but there's something else," Alerice said, glancing back over her shoulder where she could see the mossy rise and its glistening columns. "If I let the King of Shadows believe he has leverage over me, then I have the 'coin' to buy Kreston's freedom."

***

"Alerice, I wish you to end the conflict in Mortalia," the Raven Queen said. "Specifically, the conflict between your city, Navre, and the city of A'Leon."

Alerice was glad to be given the task because now she no longer needed to ask her matron's permission, for along with Kreston, the problem of Gotthard in control of Navre was forefront in her thoughts.

She stood in the Hall of Eternity at the foot of the dais. Clustered at the side of the hall near the statues of women of the arts, Alerice saw souls still waiting to be measured. Spirit guides tended to them, but Alerice knew that the queen had taken time from her sorting to summon her.

Alerice could also sense the queen's disdain for the King of Shadows, who reclined sideways on his throne. The queen could not stop a momentary glance in his direction, followed by a thin sigh as she pressed her red lips into a line. Then she focused her amethyst gaze down upon her champion.

"If all elements work according to their natures, the Realme will see benefit from this task, for which I sense your eagerness."

"I am eager, My Queen," Alerice said. "From what I was able to see on the battlefield, something has gone wrong in Navre."

The queen nodded. "Then I dispatch you."

Alerice could not help but look at the King of Shadows, who readjusted his position but did not wake from his stupor. The thought of kissing him seemed as vile as the memory of how the Reef of Navre had nearly kissed her the night he stabbed her and sent her into the Evherealme.

She needed to think of something else.

"My Queen," Alerice said. "I became practiced in one skill when I managed my Cup and Quill – forcing men to cease fighting – but I must have a strong show of force to deal with two mortals waging war. May I use the Raven Knights as I did when solving the mystery of the thief of souls?"

"You may," the queen said.

Alerice saw the Raven Knights step forward, the golden glows in their helms' eye sockets brightening. How she wished she could have opened her own dual portals to send them off.

"I need one knight to fly to Bolivar of A'Leon, and one to fly to Gotthard of Navre," she said. "I ask that both knights deliver these men to my tavern, and that you send me there so I may await them."

"Agreed," the queen said as three portals began forming within the Hall of Eternity.

***

Alerice stepped into the late afternoon sun. Golden light shone on a street lined with multi-story, exposed timber homes. She knew each door as surely as she knew each family behind it. She knew each roof as surely as she knew that the sky was blue.

She was home... and yet was she?

Alerice became aware that she stood in the open and that heads were turning in her direction. Notoriety would not serve her well at this moment, and so she turned to the narrow alley that she knew was behind her, and slipped into the shadows beside the Cup and Quill.

Her blessed shadows. She had eluded so many people in this alley. It was not lengthy, only the depth of the tavern. She touched the rock of the home next door, remembering its rough surface. She smelled the air, allowing the scent of spiced cooking and roasting meats to whisk her back to a time that seemed forever ago.

But there was work to do, and as Alerice contemplated her task, she also knew that this was no longer her world.

"Chessy?" Alerice called to her cousin, who stood thumping kegs to check their levels.

She stood inside the Cup and Quill's back door, noting that the evening crowd had not begun to arrive. Cousin Chessy looked in her direction, but she remained within the shadows, her black scales helping to conceal her.

"Who's there?" Chessy asked.

"Chessy, I want you to place a hand on the bar and grip it."

Alerice saw Chessy squint, but then he reacted as though his blood ran cold, for he obviously recognized her voice.

"God's above," he gasped. "Leecie?"

"Chessy Linden, take hold of the bar," Alerice demanded in the same voice she had used when they were teens.

Chessy's hand shot out and he did as he was told. Alerice stepped into the light spilling in from the side windows.

"Leecie!" he shouted.

"Shhh," she cautioned.

"Oh, Leecie!" he said a bit softer, bolting for her and catching her in his arms. He squeezed, but then he reacted to her scale mail tunic, and released her to look her over. "What are you wearing, and what in the world has happened to you? Are..." He gulped. "Are you Leecie's ghost? Oh, please, please tell me that's not so. You feel real. You must be real."

"It is me, Chessy, and I am alive. And if I had time to tell you everything that's happened, I would sit you down and we'd drink the kegs dry. But I don't have time, and so you're going to have to do exactly as I say." She smiled then added, "But I have been on the most amazing adventure."

The front door flew open, and two black *whooshes* flew in. Chessy's eyes went wide, but Alerice stepped around to the front of the bar.

"Place them over there," she said to the Raven Knights, who appeared in the flash of an eye, one holding Bolivar of A'Leon and one holding Gotthard of Navre. "Tavern Master!" Alerice called to Chessy. "Two tankards, and they don't have to be the best. These two don't deserve it."

The Raven Knights forced Bolivar and Gotthard to the table Alerice had indicated, and then withdrew to either side of the room. Their golden eyes glowed from the shadows created by spaces between the windows.

Gotthard and Bolivar looked about to assess their surroundings, Gotthard becoming incensed.

"What is the mean--" he tried to say.

"Gotthard," Alerice interrupted. "If you say, 'of this' I swear to the Raven Queen that I will castrate you right here, right now." She drew her Realme dagger and raised it so that it glinted with sunlight. Gotthard held his tongue. "Sit down," she ordered.

The men obeyed.

Chessy came forward with the tankards. Alerice took them and gestured her head toward the front door. Chessy nodded, and hurried to lock it. Then, he turned toward the rear door while glancing at the Raven Knights. He quickened his steps and he exited, nearly slamming the door behind him.

Alerice knew that Chessy was not running away. Rather, he was heading down the alley to the front to move out the "Tavern Closed" barrel and block anyone from entering. Sure enough, Chessy moved past the front windows, lugging something heavy, and secure in her position, Alerice was ready to manage the moment.

"You're the Ravensdaughter," Lord Bolivar said. "The one my men were telling me about."

"I am," Alerice said.

Alerice nodded to the Lord of A'Leon, but then she watched Gotthard look from the rear door to her as he likely realized her identity and her relationship to Chessy.

"It *is* you," Gotthard said. "That murderous little Linden bird."

Alerice slammed the tankards down upon the

tabletop, splashing their contents over Bolivar's and Gotthard's tunics. The men brushed off the brew, Gotthard glaring.

Alerice threw her Realme dagger into the table so that it sank into the wood. Gotthard reacted as though he had just been handed the advantage in a bar fight, but as he reached for the dagger, Alerice held her hand high, and it appeared in her palm.

"You think this is a common blade?" she asked as both men startled. "You think I wear mortal scales? You think *they* are not servants of the Raven Queen?" she asked, gesturing to the knights. "You are in the presence of a Walker of the Evherealme. Yes, me, the murderous Linden bird, whom the Reef murdered in return, and who has been to the world below and risen back into this world above. You are in my presence, in my power, and you both will now listen to me. I promise you that."

Gotthard scoffed, but Lord Bolivar rose and bowed.

"Ravensdaughter," he said with eager deference.

"Oh, shut up, Bolivar," Gotthard said, also rising. "She is Alerice Linden, the former maid of this place." Gotthard stared into Alerice's eyes. "A nothing. A nobody."

"Who poisoned you," Alerice said with a knowing grin.

Gotthard paused, giving Bolivar the chance to step about the table and come closer.

"But she appeared and disappeared on the field,"

Bolivar said. "L'Orku himself announced her. She even vanquished the--"

"Ghost of the Crimson Brigade?" Kreston said as he appeared near the bar, traces of a Realme portal vanishing behind him. He wore his gray scales, but he had left his plate and helm below.

Both Bolivar and Gotthard backed as he approached.

"Gods above," Bolivar breathed.

"You'd best say, 'Gods below'," Alerice commented. "The Crimson Ghost serves the King of Shadows as I serve the Raven Queen, and he has come to enforce my right to demand that you end hostilities immediately. The rulers of the Realme are not happy about it. This is my message to you."

"Your message," Gotthard sneered. "You will deliver no message to me. Or have you forgotten how I took you in this place?" He glanced about for the table over which he had doubled Alerice and thrown back her skirts. "Right there," he continued, pointing. "You remember the feel of me, how it must have filled you. I'm certain you recall how I had your cousin murdered right over there--"

Kreston strode forward and punched Gotthard's jaw so hard that he splayed the man to the floorboards.

Alerice saw the hate in Kreston's eyes, but she had no intention of telling him to stand down. Rather, she paced to Gotthard so that her boot rested near his head.

"Monster, I will tell you what I regret most about that moment. You took my cousin from me. You took my family from me, but more importantly, you took my good judgment from me. I regretted poisoning you, not because you didn't deserve it, but because I am a better person than that. You robbed me of my sense of self, my peace of mind, but events have a strange way of turning about, for now I have returned with such strength that I will never suffer anyone to rob me again. You are the nothing, the nobody, and if I chose to proclaim it in the streets of Navre – just as I proclaimed it on the night I gave you that cup – everyone would listen."

"It's a pity you did not kill him," Bolivar said. "Gotthard used your cup to rise against my brother. He circulated rumors that you were Andoni's spy, and extorted enough city officials that they turned a blind eye while he had Andoni murdered. This is why I've come. To rid Navre of him, which I will do now if you and the Crimson Ghost will only step aside."

"No," Alerice said flatly. "When this wretch dies, he dies publicly. If he extorted city officials and had your brother murdered, then let him stand trial for it."

"Oh, yes," Gotthard said. "I welcome a trial. Especially here in Navre."

"Where no one will convict you," Bolivar said.

Gotthard smiled. "Where no one will convict me."

"Gotthard?" Alerice interrupted in a sweetly sarcastic tone. "What makes you think the trial will be in Navre? For that matter, what makes you think it will be attended only by the living? I can guide souls up from the Realme below now. Perhaps Lord Andoni himself would like the chance to speak."

Fear shot through Gotthard's eyes. Alerice allowed it to linger before she beckoned the Raven Knights to step forward.

"I will choose the place and time to settle this matter," she said. "Until then, you two will withdraw from the field and barrack your men. If either of you advances, you will answer to me, and to my champion," she added, gesturing toward Kreston.

Kreston nodded, his expression conveying a strength that neither man dared confront.

Bolivar stood down and Gotthard looked about for a means of escape. He appeared ready to bolt for the rear door, but Kreston moved to stand in his path.

"Now," Alerice said. "Return to where you were, but always know that I have the power to summon you again."

Alerice beckoned again to the Raven Knights, who swooped in to claim their respective mortals. The tavern's front door flew open, and the knights *whooshed* out with their mortals in tow.

***

"You should have let Bolivar kill him," Kreston said. "At the very least you should have arrested him. Why'd you let him go?"

Alerice and Kreston walked along the street not

far from the Cup and Quill, the evening's dusk providing enough light by which to see. It also provided enough shadows for them both to slip in and out, no doubt creating an otherworldly effect to all who watched. They sensed many eyes upon them, though no one dared approach, save for a brief moment when Chessy had found them.

He had brought Alerice's two other cousins, Clancy and Little Judd, and Cousin Jerome's widow, Millie. Alerice had spent a short moment with them, filled with hugs and a few tears. While she promised to return to the family brewery as soon as she could, she made it clear that she and Kreston needed to walk the town to challenge Gotthard's dominion.

"If I had let Bolivar kill Gotthard," Alerice said, "which believe me was very tempting, then the Reef would control Navre, and that's not an improvement. I let them both go to make their troops stand down, but I kept Gotthard in place so Navre did not devolve into chaos. When it changes hands, I will oversee it."

"But you know he's going to plot against you," Kreston said.

"I do, but he can't harm me now, and I want everyone to know it. That's why we're taking this little stroll."

"All the same, never let your enemy have breathing room."

"What can he do, Kreston? If Gotthard killed me, the queen would restore me the way the king restores you."

"That's not something you should welcome, Alerice."

"No, but it affords me the opportunity to assert my presence as I look for someone to govern the city. It can't be Gotthard or the Reef, and if Gotthard was able to extort city officials, then they're corrupt as well. Bolivar might be the right choice. I'm going to have to meet him and see what type of man he is."

"As you say," Kreston said. "Thank the gods above that I'm a soldier, not a politician, but guard your back."

"Isn't that why I have you?" she asked with a smile. Then she softened her voice so that only he could hear. "Who told you where I was?"

"Oddwyn. I asked him when I woke up, then I asked him to send me here."

"Why?"

"To spy on you."

She hid a little laugh. "Well, if you're spying on me, why are you telling me?"

"Oh, I'm a lousy spy, but the king will want to know what you're up to. If he's not watching you through me right now, he will be soon enough. I told you once that you can't trust me. Not because of me, because of him."

She nodded, then took a breath. "Listen, Krest--"

Kreston stopped and reached out to turn Alerice toward him. "No, Alerice, you listen. You still think you can persuade the king to free me, and I'm telling you that just won't happen. He took me back. He sent me to slaughter people, and he'll do it again."

"And I'll stop you again."

"For how long?" he asked. "Alerice, we both know that the only option you think you have is to bargain with the king to free me, and what would you offer? Yourself? If you did, and if the king accepted, I am telling you right here, right now, that would destroy me."

"But..."

"No buts. I couldn't live with myself if you paid that type of price. My mistakes are my own, and I don't ask other people to clean up my messes."

She gazed into his hazel eyes, knowing there would be no use discussing her thoughts on winning a kiss from the King of Shadows. Also, he was right. Perhaps she shouldn't.

"If the king is watching, should I have you here with me?"

"As long as you don't tell me your thoughts," he said. "The king has seen us together many times, and he knows that I will try to help you no matter what he orders me to do."

"Even if he orders you to kill me?"

He paused before he said, "Even if. I defied him once and he racked my brain, but I'd go through that again if I had to."

She placed her hand on his arm.

"Then, let's make sure you don't have to. There must be a solution, Kreston."

Kreston relaxed slightly. "If anyone can find it, it's

you."

***

"Did you see her walking the streets?" Gotthard demanded.

"Yes, though I can't believe it," the Reef responded.

The two men stood in the Prime Cheval's suite, formerly Lord Andoni's domain. Gotthard had indeed taken hold of it by leveraging his having been poisoned. Since the attack had come on the night when he had hosted Andoni, he had claimed injury at Andoni's hand.

The fact that his wife, who had drunk more from the cup, had died only helped matters along. Once he recovered, Gotthard had ordered the Reef to arrest Andoni and sequester him in a cell that conveniently housed a murderer. With a simple slice of the throat, Andoni was no more, and with a proclamation by the city officials he held in his purse, Gotthard had declared himself Prime Cheval.

"I stabbed her with her own knife," the Reef said. "She died in my hold."

"I believe you," Gotthard said. "And now she claims to be the Raven Queen's daughter. She has a weird way about her. There's no denying it. So what is the solution?"

A disembodied voice spoke two simple words: "Kill her."

Both Gotthard and the Reef froze as they looked about. The suite was empty. However, the standing mirror caught their attention, for its pane began to frost over.

"Gods above," the Reef muttered.

"Or," Gotthard said, "gods below." He stepped closer to the mirror, seeing that the frost was not made of ice. Rather, it was made of tiny crystals that reflected the light from the suite's many candles.

Alerice and Kreston rode into the heart of Lord Bolivar's encampment. When they had arrived, two sentries had cried for them to identify themselves, but they had stopped short to find the Ravensdaughter and the Ghost of the Crimson Brigade.

Two pikemen had run up to escort them in, and Alerice had watched as one company after another stopped whatever they were doing to stand and stare.

The camp's fires had reflected on Kreston's gray scale mail, Jerome's flowing black mane, and Captain's mahogany shoulder as the pikemen had called for everyone to step aside. One of them had a deep voice that Alerice imagined could be heard for miles.

Lord Bolivar awaited them outside his tent, along with his marshal and other officers. Alerice glanced at Kreston for any recollection of how his men had been betrayed by their marshal, but he was his stoic self.

Burning logs in standing braziers lighted the area. Alerice and Kreston dismounted as the two pikemen held Jerome's and Captain's bridles. Alerice was about to approach Bolivar, but Kreston held her back. Then he turned to one of the pikemen and asked in a low voice, "How do you find your Lord?"

"Bolivar?" the man with the deep voice asked.

Kreston nodded, but gestured for the fellow not to speak too loudly.

The other pikeman stepped in to discretely offer, "He's a good'un, that one. Does right. Fine spine."

"Good man," the first added as quietly as he could.

Kreston patted the pikeman's shoulder. Then he turned Alerice to their waiting host even as he said under his breath, "Want to know a commander? Ask the ranks."

Alerice could not have been more grateful for Kreston's advice.

Bolivar's double-peaked tent was lighted by thick candles burning in tall holders. Several adorned his table, which was covered with maps. U-chairs bearing A'Leon's white lion on a blue field surrounded the table, while Bolivar's head chair bore the full A'Leon coat of arms.

To one side, Alerice noted a bureau topped with wine jugs and goblets. To the other she saw racks holding rolled scrolls. A scribe's desk stood near it, as did stands bearing swords and pole arms.

Alerice glanced at the maps, several of which outlined Navre's strategic positions. Bolivar gestured for her to take in her fill, which she did with calm confidence. Kreston kept to her flank, and Alerice could see Bolivar's officers doing their best to mask their realization that he was flesh, not spirit.

"You are welcome to everything, daughter of the Raven Queen," Bolivar said. "I have no secrets from the White Lady Below. My sister serves at Graystone Abbey, and she has written to me saying that the Raven's Daughter has risen to walk among us. I never imagined I would meet you, or host you at my table now, Alerice Linden of Navre."

Alerice acknowledged the familiarity, pleased at Bolivar's attempt to reach her on a personal level.

Gotthard and the Reef watched as the mirror's pane filled with smoke while a layer of tiny crystals grew thick enough to crack the glass.

Gotthard gestured the Reef back, and both men tensed as cracks ran along the mirror's surface. Then, the mirror shook on its stand until it burst forth in a shower of shards. The smoke exuded forth, and Gotthard and the Reef bolted for the far side of the suite.

The smoke swirled about in midair until it changed from gray to black, midnight blue, and deep teal.

Gotthard held his breath and the Reef swallowed hard as they saw a figure form within the swirl's center. It stepped forward, landing a white boot on the floorboards.

It was a youth with ice-blue eyes and white

hair popped with colored bursts. He wore an iridescent tunic of turquoise and lavender, accented by indigo and pearl. His shirt was crafted from some shimmering material.

He struck a pose and stared, his eyes briefly narrowing on Gotthard before he proclaimed, "Mortals, lower your gazes in awe. Bend your knees in respect, for I present to you the King of Shadows, Master of the Evherealme."

Both Gotthard and the Reef hesitated, and the youth shouted, "Kneel! Cast your eyes down!"

They gulped and complied.

Gotthard then felt an icy blast shoot up his spine, and he could not help but look up. A tall specter wearing a crystalline crown stood where the youth had been. His long gray robe was trimmed in crystals, and more crystals protruded from the shoulders.

"Come here," the specter demanded.

Gotthard and the Reef obsequiously scurried forward.

"You want to do something about the girl?" the King of Shadows asked. "Then, do as I say. Kill her."

Gotthard shook, and yet his fear was not sufficient to prevent the slight upturn of his lips.

"The murderous Linden bird," Alerice called herself.

"As I said," Bolivar commented. "It's a pity you didn't kill him. I told you I was here to do that very thing, but unfortunately your decree has left me in a difficult position."

"How so?" Alerice asked.

"I respect the gods above and below," Bolivar said. "And you have ordered me to cease my attack. This means Gotthard will go unpunished, unless you do something about it."

"As you said you would," the marshal stated. The other officers echoed his sentiment, and he folded his arms as he awaited her intentions.

"Be silent!" Kreston shouted. Alerice saw him fix a steely gaze on them before he stared at Bolivar.

"My Lord," Alerice said in a diplomatic tone. "Prime Cheval of A'Leon. I have only one question for you."

"Ask it, I beg you," Bolivar said.

"Would you keep to my decree and leave, despite what your men, or your army, or your city would think of you? Would you do this to show fealty to the White Lady Below, no matter what the personal or political cost?"

Bolivar took a breath. "I am a pious man. And so my answer must be 'yes'. It would destroy all that I have promised my people. It would mean that a guilty man lives to commit more atrocities, but..." He paused and then added with a half-bow, "I would obey, Daughter of the Raven Queen."

Alerice smiled. "Then you are the type of man who should govern Navre and bring Gotthard to account."

Gotthard's suite was the last place in Mortalia Oddwyn wished to be, and yet here he was. The King of Shadows had commanded a heraldic entrance, and Oddwyn could not deny his duty.

Yet he longed to summon Alerice's Realme dagger and cast it into Gotthard's heart, for he knew that this was the creature who had raped her.

"How do we kill her?" Gotthard asked the King of Shadows.

"The way you kill any mortal," the king said. "She is flesh, and flesh dies."

"Until the queen restores her," Oddwyn thought.

"But I did kill her," the Reef said. "And she came back."

"Exactly," Oddwyn thought.

"Lock up her soul, and her body will die," the king said.

"Ah," Oddwyn thought, for the king had just outlined what he meant to do – have one of these worms kill Alerice, and then distract the queen so that he could steal her spirit. This meant acting against his wife's champion, which meant possible war within the Realme.

"Kill the girl," the king ordered, "and I will make certain that she does not rise."

"And Bolivar too?" Gotthard asked.

"Your mortal disputes are nothing to me," the king said. "Kill whomever you wish, only kill the girl first."

"With pleasure," Oddwyn mouthed silently as Gotthard said the words aloud. He half-rolled his eyes as he watched the greedy mortals begin to plot, suddenly understanding why weak dramas inspired nausea.

"We'll invite them to a congress of truce," Gotthard said. "In the hall below, his brother's hall. That will rankle him."

"Wait," the Reef said. "What about that man of hers?"

Oddwyn caught sight of the King of Shadows, whose face almost seemed to flush. Oddwyn knew when to stand on guard, and he backed a step as the air rushed toward the Realme's master, causing the mirror shards to vibrate on the floor.

"He's not hers!" the king decreed in three distinct syllables. "He is mine. And he will remain mine until the day I let him die."

Oddwyn was rightly fearful of that tone. He watched the King of Shadows stand tall and order, "Herald!"

Oddwyn stood bolt upright. "My King."

"Go and fetch her. Fetch them all, but breathe one word of this to any mortal ear, and you will have failed me."

Oddwyn said nothing as he bowed low, a Realme portal forming at his back.

Setting a portal's course was an inherent talent for any Realme immortal. All Oddwyn required was knowledge of the person he wished to engage. The Realme provided the ether that transcended into Mortalia. There was no 'time'. There was no 'space'. There was only consciousness, and once Oddwyn knew where to aim his intentions, he directed his essence toward that location and the passageway formed – which was why he found himself quite shocked to feel some unknown hand grab hold of his tunic and pull him off course.

Oddwyn tumbled through his portal to land on the dirt outside a double-peaked tent. The black, midnight blue, and deep teal whisked off as if blown away by a stiff breeze. This place was not his intended point of entry, for he had meant to appear at Alerice's side.

Men-at-arms moved about and two guards stood at the tent's flap, but no one paid him heed, which was further strange, for Oddwyn was well aware of the figure he cut to mortal eyes.

He stood and looked about, and even waved at one of the guards. Then, Oddwyn felt a pleasant tingle run up his back, and he spun about to see two pikemen smiling at him.

Pikemen indeed.

Oddwyn beamed with joy and immediately presented her female self, for she stood in the presence of L'Orku, God of Thunder, and Gäete, God of Storms.

"Brothers!" she cried as she leaped into L'Orku's embrace.

L'Orku set his pike aside so that it stood upright of its own accord. He caught hold of Oddwyn and swept her up into his arms to plant his lips on hers. He doffed his mortal disguise to reveal himself as a brawny fellow whose red beard glistened in the torchlight, and whose mighty ram horns curled about either side of his head. Matted hair tumbled down his back, and as soon as he finished kissing Oddwyn, he tossed her to his brother.

Gäete had been strengthening the bands of silence and invisibility that protected them from mortal ears and eyes, but upon seeing L'Orku toss the Realme's herald in his direction, he likewise planted his pike upright and caught her so that he might kiss her as well.

Oddwyn caressed his smooth charcoal skin and drew strength from the tiny lightning arcs dancing about his bright eyes.

"I've always preferred you as a lass," L'Orku said in his deep, resounding voice.

"I as well," Gäete said as he tossed a giggling Oddwyn in his arms one more time. Then he spun her about as he lowered her to the ground.

Oddwyn looked over his toned body, noting the cache of lightning bolts that he wore at the back of his banded cuirass. The bolts were covered by the buckler he used to block his brother's head butts when they battled.

"What are you two doing here?" Oddwyn asked. She looked about at the encampment. "Slumming it again?"

"We enjoy slumming," Gäete said.

"When haven't you?" Oddwyn commented. "But what brings you here? You hate officers."

"Not all of them," L'Orku said. "That one is a decent man," he said, gesturing to the tent. "But we're here because of her."

"Her?" Oddwyn asked. Then the response struck her, and she asked, "You mean Alerice?"

"Very good," Gäete said with mocked applause.

"She's our girl," L'Orku said proudly. "And just look at her. What a woman. What a Walker. So accomplished in so short a time."

Oddwyn held up her hands. "Wait a moment. What do you mean 'your girl'?"

"Realme spirits," Gäete said aside to L'Orku. "Never that bright."

"Oh, give me my dice cup, and we'll see who's bright," Oddwyn said. "Now what do you mean 'your girl'?"

"We knew her father, Oddie-lass," L'Orku said. "Back when he served in Andoni's ranks. Tomas Linden. Simple soldier, simple man. He died saving his brothers in arms. He was worthy of a gift."

"So you blessed Alerice's birth?"

"L'Orku always blesses a Walker's birth," Gäete said, "but I added my own touch. Why do you think she can do things other Walkers cannot? That's my brightness inside her, despite her shadows."

"Unbelievable," Oddwyn said to herself. "But...

what now? The King of Shadows means to kill her, and I've told her that she needs his kiss to become part of the Realme."

"She has choices to make, then," Gäete said.

"And she will," L'Orku added. "She's no fool. Go to her and warn her. She'll know what to do."

"I can't. *He* won't let me."

"That shadow thinks he can trap our girl, does he?" L'Orku asked.

"He seems determined to try," Oddwyn said.

"Don't worry," Gäete said as he assumed the guise of a messenger. "I'll warn her."

"No, I will proclaim it," L'Orku said, assuming the guise of a bulky foot soldier.

"You may be loud, but I'm fast," Gäete said to his brother. "Stay here, bellow-head."

"I'll show you how to bellow," L'Orku said as he pawed the ground, produced his horns, and lowered them in his brother's direction.

Gäete conjured his buckler and held it ready, but Oddwyn jumped between the two, for if L'Orku rammed into the shield, thunder would ring out.

"Stop it, storm brains!" she demanded.

They stood down, and Oddwyn presented himself as a youth once more. He straightened his tunic and brushed off his shoulders.

"I'll go to her first," Oddwyn said. "Then you can deliver the warning," he said to Gäete. "Tell her that Gotthard has found a way to kill a Realme Walker, and tell Bolivar that Gotthard means to kill him as well. Then he'll have a reason to offer Alerice assistance."

Gäete nodded and dispelled his buckler.

"But," Oddwyn added. "Let me distract Kreston before you say anything he might overhear."

Both gods nodded, seeming to understand this necessity.

Oddwyn looked between the brothers, then winked at L'Orku before he turned and paced toward the tent, startling the guards as he slipped out from the gods' invisibility and through the flap.

**

"You wished to see me?" Alerice asked Gotthard in a sweetly sarcastic tone.

Gotthard's reaction was an astounded loss of voice, for Alerice knew that he did not plan for the show of force she had assembled in the Prime Cheval's great hall.

Daylight flooded in through the towering windows, the arched crowns of which were framed in elegantly carved stone. Ornate hammerbeam timbers rose high overhead, each the work of a master carpenter. Man-tall candelabrum dotted the walls, and man-wide chandeliers hung from the ceiling.

The Prime Cheval's chair stood on a dais at the hall's head, but Gotthard did not occupy it. Rather, he stood at one end of a long table, the Reef of Navre at his side and a cadre of men-at-arms flanking them.

Each armed man wore a blue surcoat embroidered with Navre's four gold circles. City dignitaries in formal finery stood nearby. However, every one of them was so taken aback by Alerice's company that they could do little more than stare in dumb wonder.

Kreston stood at Alerice's right, every bit the Ghost of the Crimson Brigade. Bolivar stood at her left, flanked by his marshal, officers, and a contingent of smartly dressed soldiers.

However, in preparation for what Alerice knew would be a game of 'who held the last knife', she had asked Oddwyn to help her find Lolladoe, the forest faun whom she had befriended while discovering the thief stealing souls from the Realme. Lolladoe held her crossbow ready as her hooves *clomped* on the floor stones. When she moved her head, her antler jewelry jingled.

Also present were Mutt and Wisp from the Wyld mercenary clan, their ash-and-black painted bodies striking a stark contrast to the Navre men-at-arms. Mutt growled behind the bevor plate that covered the lower half of his face, and watched the Navre men shrink from him.

Finally, Alerice had gathered two of the Painted Women, whose spirit ancestor, Pa'oula, had helped her fight the King of Shadows' monks. These copper-toned warriors bore their traditional spears while proudly displaying indigo and purple ink patterns atop shaved heads.

Alerice stood in full battle gear, save for her helm.

Still, she was terrified. She had never faced a moment where she knew someone wished to kill her, and if Gotthard had found a way to murder a Realme Walker, she could not rely on the queen's ability to restore her.

She was taking a terrible chance coming here, but killing a Walker must involve the King of Shadows. Alerice's exotic allies had already fouled any plans Gotthard had of capturing her, which would force the king to take the initiative. This was her best chance to position him for a kiss.

Alerice drew strength from the men beside her. Bolivar's life was in jeopardy, and Kreston knew that if he acted against the king he would face dire consequences. Yet neither of them showed the slightest apprehension.

And neither would she. Alerice pocketed her fear, and trusted that the little amphoras she had given Lolladoe, Mutt and Wisp, and the Painted Women would tip the balance of any metaphysical conflict.

"I hear that you seek my death," Alerice said to Gotthard. She gestured to her company. "I invite you to try."

Gotthard looked about, clearly worried that his men would be no match for her odd group.

"Do something," he commanded the Reef.

"Yes, do something," a voice demanded.

Alerice looked about for a midair distortion, for she knew that voice all too well.

A Realme portal appeared at the base of the dais.

Alerice waved for her company to fan out, which they did as several essences rushed into the hall. In moments, Lolladoe, the Wyld, and the Painted Women were under attack by unseen forces that struck them at vital body points, incapacitating them so that they fell to the floor.

Kreston drew his broadsword as he shouted, "Shadow monks!"

Alerice thought she had imprisoned these warriors after she had destroyed the King of Shadows' cliffside shrine, but he must have released them. She drew and threw her Realme dagger, knowing it would find its mark. It killed one monk, who slowed enough to be seen as he fell only paces from Lolladoe.

"At my side, Dühalde," the voice said from the dais.

Alerice watched Kreston disappear, only to reappear beside the Prime Cheval's chair. She held her hand high so that her dagger appeared in her palm, but then she felt hands upon her. She could not stop an invisible grip from forcing her to sheathe her dagger. Then it pinned her arms behind her back.

Alerice glanced at Bolivar, who was similarly apprehended, and then looked at her fallen friends. This game had taken an unexpected turn, and Alerice tried to think of what to do.

She focused on the still-open portal, which floated to the top of the dais, and then watched as the King of Shadows stepped from it.

The king raised a hand, and the shadow monk holding Alerice appeared, as did the one holding Bolivar and two more at either side of the table's head. The monks were not the problem. Alerice's crippled friends were, for if they could not reach their concealed amphoras, this plan would not work.

Alerice caught sight of Gotthard, who took a moment to process the situation before he beamed and ordered the Navre men-at-arms to surround Bolivar's company. Then he strode before the dais and bowed.

"The Ravensdaughter," Gotthard offered.

The King of Shadows struck Gotthard with a shock that propelled him to the side.

"Useless mortal," the king said as he gestured for the monk to bring Alerice forward.

She did not resist, for there was no point. There was only one question she needed to ask herself, for this was the moment of no return. Was she prepared to tether to the Realme?

Alerice looked up at the king's dark gray eyes, and forced a glimmer into her own. She nodded in a deferential challenge, despite her anxiety, and asked, "Are you certain this is a good idea, Your Majesty? The queen must be watching."

"You think I don't know how to distract my wife?" the king countered. "You think that, even from this place, I can't order the herald to babble at her while I take hold of you?"

"Oh, I'm certain Oddwyn can babble most

convincingly, Your Majesty, but why would you wish him, or her, to do that..." She allowed her voice to trail off as she used the queen's mark to project her spiritual voice, purring, *"...When you could have more of me?"*

The king looked down on her. *"I already have you, girl, for I have him,"* he said, gesturing at Kreston. *"And I will torment you with him at every turn. Your angst at his plight will be my delight. Allow me to show you."* His lips twisted into a grin, and he said aloud, "Dühalde."

Kreston tensed and looked at his master.

"Kill her," the king ordered.

Kreston looked down at her, horror flashing across his face. Then he looked at the King of Shadows, hatred mounting.

"Remember, Dühalde," the king said. "You defied me once."

Alerice saw a bolt of fear shoot through Kreston, and he closed his eyes as he steadied himself. When he opened them, he recovered his ice-hard expression and locked his stare on her.

Kreston advanced, and then paced down the dais steps. He walked toward Alerice, who wanted to tell him that she still had one more play to make in this 'last knife' game. She had told him about the plan to arrest Gotthard in his congress of truce, but she had taken his advice and not told him every detail. If only her friends could break their amphoras.

Kreston came before her. Alerice held her head

high, for he had been with her long enough to know that he should trust her. Alerice saw Kreston glance in her friends' direction, but when his gaze shifted back to her, she could not read his expression to know how they fared.

Kreston reached down to Alerice's side and drew her Realme dagger. She was about to call to her company, but he held the dagger to her throat. She drew in the words she was about to shout, trying to find the true Kreston Dühalde somewhere in his cold visage.

Kreston placed his other hand on her shoulder and gripped it tightly. He glanced once more at her company – and then he turned and launched her dagger at the King of Shadows.

"You want her dead, do it yourself, coward!" Kreston shouted. "Smash 'em!" he ordered before he lunged for the shadow monk holding Alerice.

Alerice saw the king catch her blade even as she felt the shadow monk release her. As the monk shot away so quickly that Alerice could not track him, she spun about to see her companions retrieve their amphoras as best they could and smash them against the floor stones. Then she saw them suffer more of the monks' attacks, but that would all end in the next moment.

Glistening clouds welled up, and in the blink of an eye, spirits of faun warriors, Wyld warriors, and Painted Women flew out to seize the monks.

Alerice saw Bolivar's men draw their blades upon

the Navre men, who quickly folded, given their witness to supernatural machinations. Lord Bolivar and his marshal then advanced upon Gotthard and the Reef.

Alerice held her hand high so that her dagger disappeared from the king's grip and reappeared in her palm. Then she reached out for Kreston, elated to know that not only did he trust her, he had been clever enough to discover the details of her plan without alerting the King of Shadows.

"Get below, Dühalde!" the king roared.

Alerice grabbed at Kreston's arm. "I'm coming for you," she said as a Realme portal swallowed him whole. Then the king summoned the portal to him and stepped through.

"Oddwyn!" Alerice shouted.

A new Realme portal opened, and she charged into it.

***

The King of Shadows stood over Dühalde, inundating him with visions of every mortal he had ever killed, either in the ranks of the Crimson Brigade or on independent battlefields. His Walker fell to his knees within the Hall of Misted Mirrors, screaming as he threw his palms to his skull.

Dühalde had stood in defiance once before, when he had refused his destiny as servant. The king had brought him to heel then, and as soon as he did now, he would send the Ghost of the Crimson Brigade back to Navre with an army of souls. They would destroy the city, and slaughter the residents. They would kill the one called, Bolivar, whom the girl championed, and then kill the girl's family one by one while Dühalde forced her to watch.

The king looked at his crystal-encrusted prime pane. He wished to see his wife's pet, but for some reason he could not conjure the girl's image. She was not in that Mortalia hall where he has just been forced to appear. She was not in the Realme. He considered looking into the queen's Twilight Grotto, even though he and his wife shared an unspoken bond never to invade each other's personal sanctums.

"Are you wishing to see me?" Alerice asked at the king's flank.

The King of Shadows turned about to behold the girl, a flash of astonishment in his dark gray eyes.

"Alerice..." Dühalde groaned before he doubled over.

The king glanced at him, and then saw the girl direct the boy Oddwyn to tend him. Dühalde tried to rise up on his knees, but he slumped into the herald's arms.

The king discounted them both as he turned back to the bold child standing so proudly. "You have such spirit, but what do you think you can accomplish by coming here?"

"An end to this, Your Majesty," she said flatly. "An end to your abusing Kreston, and an end to your jealous impotence."

"Girl," the king said in a measured tone, "I could show you power the likes of which you could never fathom."

"I'm sure you could," Alerice challenged. "But you'll never have what your wife has, a Walker you respect. You use Kreston to satiate your emptiness, whereas the queen uses me to reinforce what a Walker can be."

"A Walker is an instrument."

"When correctly employed," she said. "Perhaps that's why you offered me your sword, and might offer it to me again if I agreed to take it. Of course, that would mean freeing Kreston."

"No, Alerice..." Kreston moaned.

"He says no," the king commented with a grin.

"I heard him, Your Majesty, but in truth, this is not about you or me, or Kreston or the queen. It is about the Realme. It's about my place here. When I once challenged you in the field of glowing flowers, I put us at odds.

"But we do not need to be at odds. And while I want Kreston to go above and live a normal life, I want something else as well, something only you can give me. Kiss me, and you will tether me here. Kiss me, and perhaps you will have the opportunity to take pride in me."

"Damn it, Alerice!" Kreston cursed.

The king sensed the herald forcing him to stay down. Through it all, the girl remained focused.

"Otherwise, Your Majesty," she added. "How long

do you think the queen will allow you to use Kreston against me? She'll step in to cripple him again. All I need to do is distract you so she can claim him, and believe me, distracting you is *not* a difficult thing to do."

The king drew closer to Alerice, wondering what sparked her spirit. He stroked her blonde hair, for he would have her. He would also keep Dühalde, and before the girl changed her mind, the king reached to the back of her neck and drew her in. He kissed her below her ear on the opposite side of her face from where Sukaar, Father God of Fire, had kissed her, and there he held her.

Alerice felt the King of Shadows drain her breath. His kiss invaded her throat even as it invaded her soul. She hung suspended in his grasp, unable to move, unable to gasp. Yet somehow she did not feel the need to inhale or exhale. She felt the wispy smoke of his shadows fill her thoughts, and she lost track of her vision. Yet she saw things with amazing clarity.

She felt the Raven Queen's mark pulse upon her brow. She felt Sukaar's latent power rise within her breast. She felt Imari's blue crescent create inner peace – and then she felt an unstable element begin to tickle inside her ribs.

It felt like a roll of thunder. It felt like a flash of lightning, and it played within her so strongly that she began laughing.

This was joyous! Alerice felt the vastness of the

Realme enfold her. She felt the coolness of her blessed shadows bathe her. She was more than the king or the queen. She was more than the gods above. She was the Realme, it's Walker, not anyone else's, its champion, not anyone else's.

Alerice stopped laughing and opened her eyes. She reached to the king's face and stroked the beard along his jawline. He pulled away from his kiss and looked at her, and she quickly reached to the back of his neck to pulled him down and press her lips against his.

She was grateful for his gift, and she did not mind expressing it. She was grateful to have a power that might even free Kreston. She released the king, and then looked on as he backed away toward the center of his Hall of Misted Mirrors.

Alerice looked aside at an astounded Oddwyn and an agonized Kreston. She beamed at them, but then she swooned, passing into the blissfully contented sleep she could only find in this world below.

"Alerice!" Kreston called, forcing himself up. He looked at the King of Shadows, and seeing that the wretch was momentarily overwhelmed, he grabbed Oddwyn and scrambled forward.

Kreston fell to his knees at Alerice's side. He hefted her into his arms and hurriedly got back to his feet.

"Get us out of here," he demanded.

Oddwyn nodded, and quickly opened a portal.

***

Kreston laid Alerice down on the mossy rise surrounded by the silver-veined healing columns. The 'sky' above swirled in tones of deep teal with light blue currents creating a daylight hue while cascades of silvery glimmers flowed down from the columns' crowns.

He brushed Alerice's hair from her face, and though he strangled his emotions, he could not prevent his hand from trembling.

"Kreston, are you all right?" Oddwyn asked, his youthful ice-blue eyes intent upon his friend of many years.

"How would you be if you just watched the woman you love marry another man?"

"I suppose that's a good way to look at it," Oddwyn said. "She's a part of the Realme now. She'll be that way forever."

Kreston tensed to control himself, and then almost as an afterthought, he reached to his brow and felt the hated mark that the King of Shadows had scratched into his skin. He grunted in regret and then exhaled heavily.

"She didn't even win my freedom. Now that shade has us both. Why'd she do it, and why did I say 'no'? The king used it to double-back on the deal."

"The king doesn't have you both," Oddwyn said. "He has you, but not her, and now I don't think he ever will."

"What do you mean?"

"Kreston, there are other gods at work here. That's what I told Alerice earlier, and that's why she just did what she did."

"Sukaar and Imari," he said. "I know."

"But also L'Orku and Gäete. I met them in Bolivar's camp. They blessed her at birth, and now you just saw the power that gives her. The king could not resist her kiss, and she laughed at his, not derisively, but that's how he'll see it."

"And I saw what he's going to command me to do," Kreston said. "He's going to order me to kill her family. He's going to give me a soul army and order me to sack Navre and kill Bolivar."

Kreston balled his fists. "I'll stall as long as I can, but this has to end, Oddwyn. The king will deploy me against her any chance he gets, especially now if she has become as powerful as you say. If I could remove myself, I would."

Oddwyn nodded, but then both he and Kreston straightened as they felt a malevolent force invade the healing columns.

Kreston knew the sensation of the king's summons. He looked at Alerice and then at Oddwyn. "Take care of her for me."

Oddwyn grasped Kreston in a hand-to-forearm grip, both fearing this might be the last time they beheld one another.

Then Kreston vanished, leaving Oddwyn to glance down at the Realme's new Far-Walker, a mortal he knew would be able to do things according to her own volition.

"You're right, Kreston. This does have to end."

In her Twilight Grotto, where thick tree branches spreading horizontally from broad trunks outlined six window panes, the Raven Queen watched her herald move closer to her champion.

Then she glanced aside at an empty soul amphora resting on a floating stand.

***

Alerice stood on the section of Navre's city wall that crowned the portcullis. She gazed out upon the dusk landscape that streaked the clouds with orange and pink against a sea-green sky that was fading to cobalt blue.

Yesterday at this time she had walked the streets with Kreston. Now she stood awaiting his impending attack, for Oddwyn had told her everything that Kreston had said.

The King of Shadows was going to send him to Navre with a soul army. He was going to force Kreston to slay her family, which was why Alerice had gathered them in the Prime Cheval's great hall.

Her cousins, Chessy, Clancy, and Little Judd, had all wanted to fight, still beside themselves with wonder at what she had become. However, Alerice had asked them to protect Uncle Judd, Aunt Carol, Cousin Millie, and Grammy Linden. Fortunately the boys had seen the sense in her plan.

Of course, Alerice was not about to leave her family so thinly guarded, especially given that the coming fight would involve elements of the Realme, and so she had asked Lolladoe, Mutt, Wisp, and the two Painted Women to also protect her family. She had helped them all recover from the shadow monks' attacks, and they were more than ready for action.

So too were the remaining spirits who possessed the stamina to sustain themselves in Mortalia throughout the day. These included Ketabuck and a few of his faun warriors, all of whom were happy to reunite with Lolladoe and once again behold their clan's precious gem, the Heart of the Forest.

It included Pa'oula, the Painted Woman, and a few of her sister spirits. They floated stoically with spears at the ready near their mortal offspring, none of them making a fuss, for Painted Women were keen on battle.

As for the shadow monks, Alerice had sent them to the Raven Queen via the very first portal she had created herself, and what an amazing moment that had been.

Her portal had been ringed in plum and lapis, not the traditional black, midnight blue, and deep teal. She had formed it by extending her consciousness to where she had wished to travel, and then simply allowing herself to slip through. She knew that the Raven Queen's mark upon her brow guided her, but so did Imari's crescent. She knew that Sukaar's power propelled her, but so did the King of Shadows' kiss.

And then there was the unknown feeling that had tickled her ribs and made her laugh. Oddwyn had explained that the brother gods, L'Orku and Gäete, had blessed her birth, and the feeling was their gift. However, she was not certain how to process this contribution, and so she tucked it to the back of her thoughts.

Alerice gazed down at the A'Leon encampment which now surrounded Navre's gates. Lord Bolivar had arrested Gotthard and the Reef. He had taken possession of the city and organized his troops outside to await any approaching foes, but what good would they be against an army of souls?

And for that matter, what good would Bolivar be?

Alerice turned and glanced down inside Navre at the decorative cobblestone courtyard that fanned out before the Prime Cheval's hall. Lord Bolivar waited there, along with his officers and a cadre of his best soldiers. A pike regiment stood at the rear of his company. Two of the men caught Alerice's eye, even from such a distance, for they had offered her some interesting advice.

They had said that spirits who died in the world above stayed dead. They never returned to the Realme, and so Alerice should take care if she shot one with her crossbow, for shooting a wicked soul would be just. However, she must use every ounce of intuition to know if the soul was wicked, lest she shoot a soul that was being unjustly used against her.

It was a sagacious offering from two common pikemen, and Alerice wished Oddwyn had been present to confirm their counsel. However, Alerice had not seen the Realme's herald since leaving the healing columns. Perhaps because the Raven Queen wished for her to stage this fight alone. Perhaps because she had just transcended the Realme to become a Far-Walker, as Oddwyn had put it.

Whatever the reason, Alerice hugged her feathered cloak, for she had never felt more alone. She looked at the final ray of sunlight disappearing behind the distant hills, and then she looked down upon the field outside of Navre's gates. Kreston Dühalde stood there in full scales, plate, and helm, the very image of the Ghost of the Crimson Brigade.

Alarm horns blew within the encampment, and soldiers rushed toward Kreston's position. Without pause, Kreston drew the King of Shadows' broadsword and began doing what he unfortunately did all too well – killing anyone who came within range.

Alerice quickly glanced back at Bolivar and his men. She saw them reacting to the horns. She did not know if they meant to break ranks and rush out to help their soldiers, but she needed them to remain in place. Besides, she had armed them all with soul amphoras that they would deploy to tip the balance of any metaphysical conflict.

Alerice made a show of spreading her cloak so that her black silhouette stood out against the darkening sky, and as soon as it formed into wings, she launched herself and shot for Kreston.

Alerice *whooshed* past the Crimson Ghost so closely that she easily pushed him off-balance. Just as in yestermorning's battle, he recovered and looked about for her, but she had already circled and beat her cloak's wings solidly to swoop down toward him again.

She watched him focus on her and raise his sword to strike, but she darted hard to the side just before reaching him, and he sliced into thin air. Then she darted aside once more to begin circling him.

With one wingbeat after another, Alerice pushed all nearby men off their footing. Some stumbled backward. Others fell onto their rumps.

Then she alighted and appeared, standing tall as the captain from yestermorning's cavalry rode up, flanked by his mounted men.

Alerice looked up at them, and then leveled her sights on Kreston.

"Stand down, Crimson Ghost!" she demanded in as loud a voice as she could muster. "There is no slaughter for you here!"

Kreston readied his broadsword, but said nothing. Alerice could see his hazel eyes narrow behind his helm's angular slits, and watched him snarl through what she could see through the vertical slit.

She glanced about at the A'Leon soldiers, quickly assessing that they looked emboldened by her command, and the last thing she wanted was to inspire them to cut Kreston down.

Alerice looked up at the mounted captain and ordered, "Keep your men away! No one stands against the Crimson Ghost save me, the Raven Queen's daughter!"

"Aye, Black Lady!" the captain replied before he began barking orders for the soldiers to clear off.

Alerice watched them provide a great deal of room, and then looked at Kreston. She saw the mark of the King of Shadows glow upon his brow, and then heard his mental voice.

"Gods, I love you, Alerice."

She smiled, though she still stood tall.

"Take the city, if you can!" she challenged, mostly to extract him from the moment. "Bolivar and I await you."

"How I wish you didn't," he said before he turned aside and began pacing toward the Navre portcullis.

Alerice spread her cloak once more as the evening drew in, the beat of its wings creating a downdraft that inspired the soldiers to give Kreston a wide berth.

In his Hall of Misted Mirrors, the King of Shadows beheld his Walker within his crystal-encrusted pane. The girl was ready for his advance into Navre? So be it. Dühalde would have his army of souls, and the king had some specific souls in mind. He focused his remaining mirrors into different locations within the Realme to fetch them.

Kreston stood before the barred entrance to the waiting city. The great bolted timbers of the portcullis would only hinder him for a moment, for the king would surely grant him passage via portal. His army would enter any way they pleased.

And if Alerice had any sense, she would use that Realme crossbow of hers and shoot down every soul in rapid succession. The King of Shadows would no doubt send the worst of the worst to terrorize the city. They would hurl themselves into homes and make away with babes. They would wreak havoc in the night. The less of them the better, and if he could he would assist in slaying them himself.

Kreston tensed, for he sensed the advance of the king's ranks. Still looking ahead, he saw a distant Alerice alight within the city entrance and move inward toward what Kreston knew from walking with her yesterday would be the courtyard at the Prime Cheval's hall.

If that was where he must confront her, so be it. If that was where Bolivar waited, all the better.

Kreston passed his broadsword into his left gloved hand and reached to his left shoulder. The red scales upon his shoulder still felt intact, even though he had loosened them enough that all he had to do was twist a few and pull hard to snap them off their rings.

Kreston looked up as firepits along the city walls came to life. Then, he felt a presence to his right and looked aside to see a lordly soul floating next to him. Kreston's brow furrowed inside his helm, for this was not a wicked man raised from the Realme's dregs.

"Who are you?" he asked.

The spirit looked longingly at the Navre portcullis. "I am Lord Andoni of House Anzar," it replied.

"Andoni?" Kreston questioned, until he realized what was happening. "You're Bolivar's brother."

"I am," the soul said in a forlorn voice.

"Gods above," Kreston said, despite the need to maintain his battle countenance. "The king sent you to break Bolivar's will."

The soul did not respond, and in the next moment the ghost of an infantry man appeared at Andoni's flank.

"And you?" Kreston asked.

The ghost looked at Kreston, but then saw the spirit of his liege, and bowed to it. Andoni acknowledged the ghost, who turned and stood at attention.

"I asked, who are you?" Kreston repeated.

"Tomas Linden, at your service," the ghost replied.

Kreston paused, but then his blood ran cold. "You're... her father."

"Captain?" a voice questioned from Kreston's

opposite side.

Kreston stood upright, for he knew that voice. He could not help but spin about, only to behold his brother-in-arms from the Crimson Brigade, his lieutenant, Landrew Mülton.

Landrew stood proudly and saluted. "Where do you want the men, sir?"

Kreston gulped, for he felt his army fill in behind him, and his worst fears were confirmed when he turned about to behold the entire Crimson Brigade.

That loathsome wretch! The King of Shadows had served up the spirits of men Kreston held most dear, spirits he had never sought out all these years walking the Realme for fear he would lose his mind if he ever beheld them.

And now they stood ready for him to order them into the waiting defenses of the woman he loved and the death she would no doubt give them.

Kreston had not tasted the salt of tears in ages, and yet he tasted them now.

Kreston reached to his red scales and snapped off enough to create an adequate chink. Then he tossed the King of Shadows' broadsword back into his right hand, raised it, and shouted, "Into the city!"

In his Hall of Misted Mirrors, the King of Shadows summoned his two Shadow Warriors and bade them to enter Mortalia. The warriors drew their broadswords and flew into the king's prime pane to execute their task.

On the courtyard's torchlit cobblestones, Alerice stood before Bolivar and his men. She glanced behind her at the candlelight shining from the Prime Cheval's hall's great windows, and knew that both the mortals and souls guarding her family were prepared.

Alerice looked at the men behind her, seeing that all eyes were fixed on her. She found the two pikemen who had given her advice, and nodded to them. Then she heard the otherworldly sound of howls on the evening air, and watched the spine-curdling effect it had on Bolivar's troops.

"Your amphoras," Alerice shouted as she removed the one she wore about her own neck from inside her scale mail tunic.

"Do as the Raven's Daughter says," Lord Bolivar ordered, reaching to the amphora he had tucked inside his vambrace.

Alerice watched his men follow suit, and then focused on the shadows, sensing the influx of a phantasmal army. She held her fist high, and then cast her amphora to the cobblestones.

It shattered, freeing the spirit inside. A glimmering essence rose up as Alerice heard several amphora smashes behind her, and she watched Aric, elder of the Hammer Clan, take shape before her. She saw him glance behind her, which prompted her to turn, and as more essences rose up, members of the Hammer Clan began floating above the cobblestones.

Alerice looked back at Aric, who nodded in response. Then she took hold of her Realme crossbow in one hand and the edge of her cloak in the other and shouted, "Kill only the wicked! Hold the rest for me!"

With his own otherworldly howl, that Alerice sensed bolstered Bolivar's men, Aric and the Hammer Clan launched themselves at the invading spirits, and in no time the ethereal *clang* of war hammers upon broadswords echoed through the city streets.

Alerice was prepared to act either offensively or defensively when she saw a stately soul walk forward into the torchlight. She paused, confused, for she knew its face. It was Lord Andoni, and he was walking toward his brother. Alerice wanted to shout a warning to Bolivar, for as the man locked eyes with his dead sibling, he became too overwhelmed to move.

However, just then another ghost caught the corner of Alerice's eye. She reflexively raised her crossbow as her head snapped in its direction, but she, too, stopped short.

"Da?"

A Shadow Warrior swooped into the Prime Cheval's great hall and landed before the assembly of mortals and spirits. The Linden women shrieked in spite of themselves, and the Linden men quickly stood before them.

Lolladoe fired a crossbow bolt into the warrior's breastplate, but it passed through and shot a hole in one of the great windows' panes. The faun spirits bared their antlers and the souls of the Painted Women bared their spears, and both groups launched forward to battle the shade. However, no force, physical or metaphysical, could slay a Shadow Warrior.

Drawing its broadsword, the warrior slew Pa'oula with a single stroke and then slew Ketabuck in a riposte.

Lolladoe blinked in horror, and then fired another bolt into the Shadow Warrior's empty helm. It passed through as before, but the faun then drew a breath and bugled at the top of her lungs.

Lolladoe's voice rang in Alerice's ears, drawing her attention away from her father's ghost. She turned to the commotion inside the hall, fearing for her family's safety.

She was about take flight to them when a thrown broadsword cut through her father, rendering him into a soft dust that filtered away into the evening breeze.

Alerice could not hide her alarm as she looked about for Kreston, only to watch the same broadsword cut down Andoni's soul as it reached out for Bolivar.

"Kreston!" Alerice cried.

To her side, Kreston stepped forward from the shadows. He wore no helm, and the look of utter loss commanded his expression.

Alerice watched him look about at the sight of his apparitional soldiers in the custody of the Hammer Clan.

"Kill them, Alerice," he said. "Kill them all."

Alerice saw one younger soul fly in toward Kreston, and noted that he bore an officer's uniform. On it, she saw the patch of two crossed red swords, and knew he was a member of the Crimson Brigade.

"Captain?" the soul asked.

"Hold your place, Landrew," Kreston said.

Alerice watched the young officer stand at attention, but then she saw a tear fall from Kreston's eye as he held his hand high so that the king's broadsword would appear in his palm.

"No, Kreston!" Alerice shouted as she took flight. She caught hold of Landrew's soul, and tucked it within the folds of her feathers. Then she darted about the courtyard collecting all the souls held for her by the Hammer Clan.

The clan had killed none. Therefore, none of them could be wicked – and all of them bore the patch of the Crimson Brigade. Why was Kreston leading his own men against Navre? Why had he been about to kill the lieutenant she knew he still held dear?

One of the king's Shadow Warriors alighted at the courtyard's center and *shrieked* into the night.

Bolivar and his men recoiled, but Kreston turned to face the monster. To her side, Alerice caught sight of the other Shadow Warrior threatening her family within the hall.

There was only one thing to do. "My Queen! Your knights!"

In her Twilight Grotto, the Raven Queen looked at her Raven Knights. She nodded to them, and they cawed as they spread their winged cloaks, vanishing as they took flight.

The queen then looked at the maiden Oddwyn, who gazed up at her with plaintive, ice-blue eyes.

Then, the queen looked at the empty soul amphora cupped in her palms.

Alerice watched as the sky above began to swirl with the Realme's tri-colors of black, midnight blue, and deep teal. A portal opened and the queen's two Raven Knights flew out and down, one confronting the Shadow Warrior in the courtyard and the other diving for the warrior inside the hall.

Alerice noted their immortal combat, and though she briefly considered that the contest of these servants of the Realme's master and mistress might bode true war for the Evherealme, she tucked that notion away and beat her cloak's wings to return to Kreston.

She alighted before him, knowing she should feel betrayed.

"Kreston, why did you kill my father?"

"Because the king sent him here to torment you," he said. "That's why you never seek out loved ones in the Realme. It eats at your mind and heart. The king sent your father to torment you, just as he sent

Andoni to torment Bolivar, and Landrew to torment me... and me to torment you." He paused and then said, "This is over, Alerice. Now give me Landrew so I can spare him."

"No, I will spare him, and protect him, and I will have the king release you if it's the last thing I do."

"Then gods above damn you, Alerice Linden!" Kreston shouted as he raised his broadsword and cleaved for her blonde head. Alerice dodged, but Kreston spun about to cleave at her side. His stroke caught her in the scales and knocked her off-balance, and he pressed his attack by striking her across the back to splay her down to the cobblestones. He kicked her in the gut to roll her over, using his strength to deny her the opportunity to draw and activate her pixie poles.

Alerice nimbly rolled away and got to her feet, but then she saw Bolivar summon his officers and hurry forward. They would flank Kreston if she did not do something.

A tactic jumped to mind, and though she had no idea if it would work, she decided to test a Far-Walker's strength.

She closed her eyes and gave every ounce of herself over to what she knew she had become: the beloved daughter of the Raven Queen and Imari, the passionate object of Sukaar and the King of Shadows, and even the god child of L'Orku and Gäete. Then she sprang upward at Kreston to wrap her arms about his body even as she demanded that her wings beat as hard as they possibly could. She felt a powerful gust blow into them from below, lifting them both high, almost as though Gäete himself had sent a breath of stormy wind to aid her.

Alerice landed once more atop the section of city wall that crowned the portcullis. Unable to hold Kreston a moment longer, she dropped him, but then toppled toward the side of the wall.

Someone grabbed the scruff of her scale mail tunic and drew her back from the brink. Then that same someone tore her cloak off her body and cast it to the ground below. She watched it float down, but then felt Kreston grab her arm and spin her about.

He locked stares with her – and then dropped his broadsword to the stones. As it clanked to rest, Kreston grabbed hold of Alerice's left arm and held her in an iron grip. Then he forced his left hand over her right, and guided her palm over her dagger's handle.

With a quick tug, he drew the blade and closed her fingers over the handle, his gloved hand holding hers.

"I said this is over."

"Yes," she said. "I'll yield if that's what you need."

"No," Kreston said, forcing her to lift the dagger and aim its tip at the chink in his red scales. "Kill me."

Alerice mouthed the word, "What?", her eyes imploring him to change course.

"Do it now," he said. "Before that wretch puts me back in action. He'll have Oddwyn restore me, and if there is any mercy the queen will lock my brain away again."

He moved the tip into his armor, and Alerice felt the resistance of his body. She saw him wince, but then she saw him beg for her to act. In that moment, she knew it would be better for him never to have known her, never to remember her once he woke within the healing columns, for if the King of Shadows would not grant him liberty, she would.

"I will see you free, Kreston Dühalde."

He smiled. "If anyone can it's you."

Though Alerice knew that her steel had already pierced his flesh, she watched as Kreston drew close and kissed her with every ounce of his pent-up passion.

He released her arm, and she grabbed hold of his shoulder. Then, she thrust her dagger into him, feeling it drive as deeply as the Reef of Navre had driven her own dagger into her heart not so very long ago.

"Now, Oddwyn," the Raven Queen ordered in her Grotto.

The maiden Oddwyn conjured a portal and disappeared.

"I should have known!" the King of Shadows shouted at the foolish scene playing out in his prime pane. Both it and the other eleven mirrors shook in their smokey tendrils, but just as the king was about to summon the Realme's herald to fetch Dühalde's body, the girl Oddwyn appeared to his left.

"Go and bring him, herald," the king ordered. "That child thinks she can help the queen lock his mind away again, but I'm not about to let that happen a second time."

"Yes, but My King?" Oddwyn said, perhaps a little too sweetly.

"What?" the king asked.

"You see, the queen... She has asked me to... You see..."

In her Twilight Grotto, the Raven Queen conjured the sight of the Convergence in one of her windows. Kreston's spirit appeared there, looking about for his body. The queen curled her willow-white fingers into the palm of one hand while holding the soul amphora in the other.

Kreston's soul flew through the window to her. She caught hold of it, and gently directed it into the amphora, managing every moment of its glistening descent.

"The queen what?" the King of Shadows demanded.

The maiden Oddwyn curtseyed deeply so that her knees touched the floor, but looking into the king's dark gray eyes, she rose back up and stood with her shoulders back.

"The queen commanded me to do something."

"Well, what is it?"

Oddwyn paused one final moment and then said,

"Distract you, My King."

The King of Shadows thought the command curious, until he spun about and looked into his prime pane at the sight of the child kneeling beside his fallen Walker.

Alerice withdrew her dagger from Kreston's side and looked about. All she could see were storm clouds rolling in against the moonlight. Fires burning along the wall highlighted Kreston's body, and she could see the blood trailing across his gray scales. But she saw nothing else.

"Where are you, Oddwyn?" she called into the night. "Oddwyn!"

She felt Kreston's face. It was cold, and his complexion was growing pale. The clouds above moved with surprising speed, and she looked about once again.

"Oddwyn!" she called again.

Lightning split the night, and Alerice recoiled. When she looked up, she saw the King of Shadows standing over her.

"She's not coming," the king said. "He's not coming. Neither of them are coming. My wife has Dühalde's soul. He's dead."

Alerice looked at Kreston in disbelief. Then the truth struck her, and she felt a flash of anger as she scrambled to her feet. She raised her bloody dagger against the king, but then she caught sight of Kreston's broadsword.

As another bolt of lightning flashed and a clap of thunder rolled out, Alerice tossed her dagger aside, swept the sword into her grasp, and aimed it at its master.

"So now you claim my blade," the king said, the crystals on his crown and standing out from his shoulders seeming to reflect the after-traces of the lightning above.

"Yes, I do," Alerice said, her expression hardening. "But not in your service. The gods above and you below have blessed me, and I am no longer yours. I am the Realme's."

"I am the Realme," the king said.

"No, you and your wife are the personifications of the Realme, but you are not the world below. It is boundless, and you are fixed, and I will walk past you both. I will carry this sword with me – though I will never draw it again. I will never allow you to enslave anyone else with it again. This is the last time you will ever see its service. I promise you that."

"And how do you think you can accomplish all this?" the king asked.

"With a little bit of help," two voices said – L'Orku in his deep, rolling tone and Gäete in his higher tenor.

The three immortals locked stares before L'Orku lowered his torso and presented his great ram horns. Then he charged at the King of Shadows, colliding with him so soundly that thunder rang out atop the wall as he sent the king toppling off into the night.

Gäete reached out to steady Alerice from the

percussive shock. As she grabbed hold of his arm, he reached out with a charcoal hand to touch the broadsword. His lightning-ringed eyes danced as he ran his fingers up the blade from hilt to tip, causing it to crackle with living dynamic.

Gäete then smiled at Alerice, who looked at the sword's many arcs before she looked up at the brother gods. Then she stood upright before them and raised the blade in salute, her back straight as she lowered her weight onto her rear leg in her classic reverence.

"Do use it," Gäete said. "Use it well."

Alerice nodded, but then she looked down at Kreston's body. There was only one proper way to send him off, and so she raised the lightning blade high so that it danced in the night sky. Then she brought it to her, turned its point down, and slammed it through the heart of Kreston's gray scales.

A blast flashed brightly, and yet this time Alerice did not feel any repercussion. She saw a brilliant wave spread out from Kreston's body, and though she needed to glance away for a short moment, when she looked down, Kreston's body was gone – as were both L'Orku and Gäete.

**

Alerice stood atop a small rise that was capped by a little shade tree. Stretching out before her was a flat expanse where two mornings ago, two armies had joined battle. Kreston had stood beside her then, and she had promised him she would be his advocate.

Now, the battle was done. Lord Bolivar was now the official Cheval of both Navre and A'Leon. He had ordered his men to clear the field and bury the dead. Alerice could see the mounds where groups of men lay.

She stood quietly in her black scales. She bore no gorget or plate. Her Realme dagger rested at her hip, opposite her crossbow. Her pixie pole cylinders hung from her belt, but she now bore another belt – a man's belt, Kreston's belt.

Strapped to it was the sheath of the broadsword he had been forced to bear. The weapon was hers now, and she intended to keep her vow that the King of Shadows would never again use it to enslave someone.

The king would likely find another champion in time. There were always men willing to seek him out, but Alerice doubted he would ever find another natural Walker. As so many others had told her, her kind was not born all that often. The king might seek one out, but Kreston Dühalde had been a unique fellow, a combination of talent in both the worlds above and below, and yet a man driven to try and right the wrongs he had suffered.

A small red bird alighted on one of the little shade tree's branches. It sung a moment, and then cocked its head to spy down on Alerice. She smiled as she gazed upon it, and then watched as it looked into the distance and darted away.

Then Alerice saw a Realme portal begin to open beside her, and she looked once more upon the field.

A youthful Oddwyn appeared and lifted his hand in salutation. Alerice saw him from the corner of her eye, but did not acknowledge him. She waited for him to approach, which he did. He held something in his hand, but she did not look closer to see what it was.

"I..." Alerice paused before she said, "I should have let myself love him more, Oddwyn. He deserved it. He was a good man who suffered bad things. He should have had a better life."

"It's always sad when mortals don't get the life they long for, but that's the way things often happen. You gave him what love you could. He wanted more for a while, but resigned himself in the end. And you did give him love. And he knew that."

Alerice thought of Kreston's hazel eyes and the way he laughed when he was truly himself. Her tears began to well up, and she closed her eyes to think of something else.

"Did you take my cloak back to the Realme so what's left of the Crimson Brigade could be safely placed?"

"I did," Oddwyn said.

"And Lolladoe, and Mutt and Wisp, and the Painted Women?" she asked.

"All back where they belong. We can always go seek them out, if you like, both here and below."

"Perhaps we will," she said.

"Perhaps you will," he offered. "When I said we, I meant as walk-about friends. You don't need me any longer."

"No," she said before she drew and released a deep breath. "Before she sent me to Navre, the Raven Queen said that if all elements worked according to their natures, then the Realme would see the benefit. But what benefit, Oddwyn? Losing Kreston is a benefit to the queen, I suppose, because the king can't use him against me any longer, but the queen has lost me too, in a way."

"Hmmm," Oddwyn mused, looking Alerice over. "And yet you still wear her scales."

"But I choose to," Alerice said most heartfully.

"Then perhaps that's another benefit. The queen has a colleague in you now, and so does the Realme."

"Mmmm," Alerice said. "It's always been about the Realme for me, hasn't it."

"I'd say so," Oddwyn said, a twinkle in his ice-blue eyes.

"Do you think, then, that the queen knew all this would happen?" Alerice asked.

"I don't know. I told you, it's not my place to know her mind."

Alerice nodded.

"So, what's it like?" Oddwyn asked sweetly, presenting her maiden form. "I've never met a Far-Walker."

"It's... strange," Alerice said, reaching out to take her Realme sister's hand. "Sometimes, I feel the full might of each immortal working together within me. Sometimes, if I concentrate, I can call upon each immortal separately, though I doubt I'll ever call upon the king or the shadows he commands."

Oddwyn patted Alerice's hand, and then presented himself as a youth once more to tuck the item he was holding into her palm.

Alerice looked down to find Kreston's soul amphora, and she gulped back a sob. Then, she curled her fingers about its smooth surface and held it tightly.

"You can always wear it," Oddwyn offered.

"No," she said. "That will only tempt me to open it and see him again. He's gone, Oddwyn. He wanted an end to this, and now he has it. Let's let him be." She turned to Oddwyn and asked, "Yes?"

"Yes," Oddwyn said.

Alerice smiled and closed her eyes. While holding the amphora in one hand, she reached down to release her crossbow with the other. Then she concentrated on Imari's blue crescent that wove into the Raven Queen's mark upon her brow.

A pleasant breeze blew in, warming the morning air with a gentle perfume. Then a low fog swelled about the field, covering the mounds.

Alerice opened her eyes and watched the two layers play against one another, the wind churning up the top of the mist so that it looked like some apothecary's preparation.

Alerice allowed a few moments to pass, and then

she raised her crossbow and took aim at the distance. The bow string pulled back of its own accord, and a gleaming black bolt appeared in the flight groove.

"Throw it," Alerice said as she passed the amphora to Oddwyn.

Oddwyn took it, and then hurled it as far as he could. Alerice took aim and fired.

The bolt struck home, shattering the amphora in midair. Alerice felt Oddwyn come next to her and snuggle a bit as she watched the amphora's contents cast the field with a glistening cascade.

The wind scattered the evanescent particles about so that they dusted the top of the mist, and then the wind blew in just a bit more to waft the mist away.

As Alerice looked out, she saw that new grass had begun to sprout on the field. Also tiny little ground scrubs had begun to grow, each of which bore clusters of miniature red flowers.

Alerice could not stop the tears from rolling down one cheek and then the other. Oddwyn balled his iridescent sleeve into his hand, turned her toward him, and wiped them from her face. Then he tickled his fingertips along the jawline scar left by Sukaar, Father God of Fire.

Alerice sniffed, and then ran her own black sleeve across her face. She reattached the crossbow to her belt, and found her hand naturally curling about the handle of Kreston's broadsword.

Oddwyn smiled, and opened a small portal beside them. As when riding along the ridgeline after giving

Alerice her black hat, he reached into the vertical slit, diving deeply so that his arm disappeared up to his shoulder.

"Ah… ha!" he exclaimed as he withdrew two foaming tankards and handed one to Alerice. "To you, Dühalde," he said, raising his.

"To you, good friend," Alerice said, raising hers.

Together, she and Oddwyn lowered their tankards, poured a bit of brew out onto the ground, and then touched rims before they drank.

Alerice savored the flavor, for it was rich and pure as she knew any Realme nourishment would be from this moment forward. When she finished drinking, she saw Oddwyn looking at her lovingly.

"You wanna go below?" he asked. "The Hammer Clan is having another feast. Lots more brew."

Alerice smiled, then gave her full concentration over to visiting the mead hall, where she knew Aric and his kindred spirits would be happy to see her. Her portal opened in a swirl of plum and lapis, and she found no difficulty maintaining it in the mortal world.

"After you, Oddwyn," she said.

"Hmmm, race you for it." Oddwyn presented herself as a maiden one final time to say, "Last one there buys!"

Oddwyn charged into the portal. Alerice looked after her confusedly.

"Oddwyn, they're free," she said before she smiled to herself. She paused and raised her tankard once more before saying, "Gods above bless and keep you, Captain Dühalde."

Then she strode into her portal, calling, "We'll see who pays!"

Tales of the Ravensdaughter

will continue with
Collection Two

To play out Collection One, please search for
"Summon Your Courage" by the Steel City Rovers.

PLEASE REVIEW THIS BOOK:

If you enjoyed *The Raven's Daughter*, please leave a review.

AMAZON

GOODREADS

AUTHOR'S WEBSITE

Thank you and blessings,
Erin Hunt Rado
ErinRadoAuthor.com

BOOKS IN THIS SERIES

*Tales of the Ravensdaughter
- Collection One*

The Beast Of Basque

The Thief Of Souls

The Wizard And The Wyld

Rips In The Ether

Mistress Of Her Own Game

The Raven's Daughter

Made in the USA
Columbia, SC
30 October 2022

70223948R00054